Angelcake

by Rodney Peppé

One winter's day, Angelmouse and Quilly were making a snowangel in the garden.

"Just one thing wrong. No thingamajig," said Angelmouse. "He can have mine!"

Suddenly, the snowangel
became a real angel!
"Message for Angelmouse,"
he said. And just as he handed the
note to Quilly, he disappeared!

"It's from You-know-who," said Quilly.
"It says: **You must get a special cake for
Elliemum's tea.**"
"That's easy-peasy," said Angelmouse.
"We'll go to Little Petal's shop."

"There's your cake," said Little Petal.

"It doesn't look like a special cake," Angelmouse complained.

"Say thank you," said Quilly, nudging Angelmouse.

"Thank you!" said Angelmouse, rather rudely.

As Angelmouse and Quilly flew with the cake,
they heard Oswald's plane.

"Look out!" cried Quilly
as Oswald screeched past them.

"No air brakes! No air brakes!"

"Look where you're going!" shouted Angelmouse.

But it was too late. He had
dropped the cake!

Angelmouse and Quilly looked for the cake all over the village. But they couldn't find it anywhere.

They asked Spencer if he had seen it.

"Was it in a tin?" he asked.

"Yes!" squeaked Angelmouse. "Have you seen it?"

"It was rolling down the hill towards Hutchkin's burrow," said Spencer. "Going at quite a speed, don't you know."

"We'll ask Hutchkin," said Angelmouse.
"I hope he's in," gulped Quilly.

"Mmm – nice," said Hutchkin as the two friends came in.

"Hello," said Angelmouse. "Have you seen a cake?"

"Seen it, man? I ate it," Hutchkin grinned. "It was a carrot cake, man. Like, it just rolled into my burrow."

"You ate it **all?**" asked Angelmouse.

"Gone, man," replied Hutchkin. "All gone!"

"What am I going to do now?"
groaned Angelmouse. "You-know-who
said I had to take a cake to Elliemum."
  "I've got an idea!" suggested Quilly.
  "You could bake one yourself. Come on!
I'll help you."

So the two friends began to make a cake. Angelmouse stirred the mixture with his tail. But he was making such a mess, that Quilly had to give him a spoon.

"It doesn't look much like a cake to me," said Angelmouse.
"That's because it hasn't been baked yet," explained Quilly.

"That's what we have to do next," said Quilly.
Angelmouse put the cake mixture into the oven. Then the
two friends waited and waited for the cake to bake.

A little while later, Angelmouse and Quilly carefully took the cake out of the oven. But it didn't look like the kind of cake Elliemum would like.

"Oh no! That's not a special cake!" cried Angelmouse.

"It's all gone wrong, and now it's too late!"

As a tear ran down his cheek, Angelmouse's thingamajig dropped onto the cake. It did a magical, thingamajig thing!

"Look, Angelmouse!" cried Quilly, "It **is** a special cake!"

"Yes, it is. It is a special cake, a special **angelcake!**" declared Angelmouse. "And we've still got time to take it to Elliemum for tea."

Soon, Elliemum's house was in sight.

"Oh! Everyone's here. This is a surprise,"
declared Elliemum, as the friends sat down for tea.
"Back in a minute."

Elliemum looked in the cupboard. She was very sad.

"No biscuits, no buns," said Elliemum to herself.

"What **am** I going to do? I've got nothing to give them."

Just then, there was a knock at the door.
"Not more guests," wailed Elliemum.

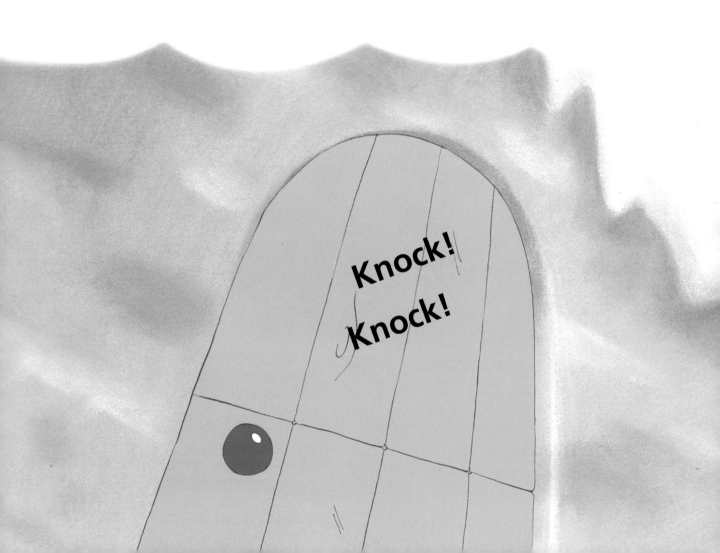

Elliemum opened the door to find a huge cake on the step.

"Special delivery for Elliemum," said a little voice
from behind the cake.

"Angelmouse, is that you?" Elliemum asked.

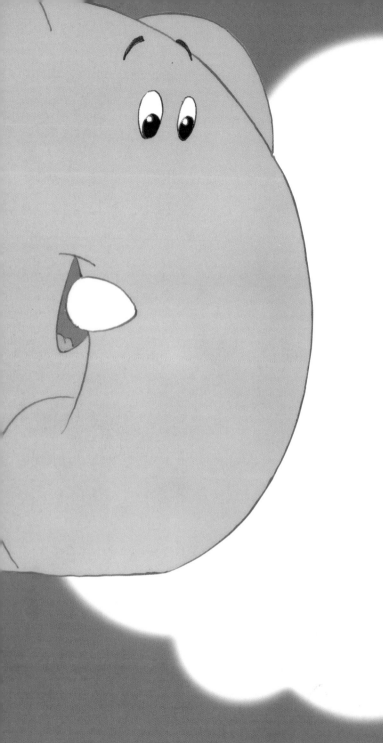

It was little
Angelmouse!
When Elliemum
saw who was behind
the wonderful cake,
she exclaimed,
"You're an angel,
Angelmouse!"

Angelmouse and Quilly joined their friends for tea.
Everyone agreed that the angelcake was the best they
had ever tasted.

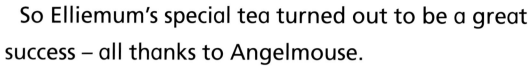

So Elliemum's special tea turned out to be a great success – all thanks to Angelmouse.